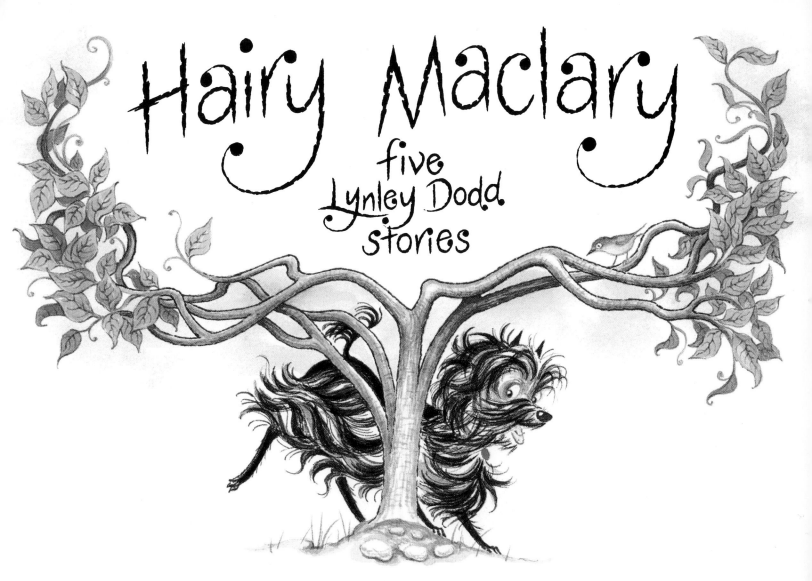

Hairy Maclary

five Lynley Dodd stories

PUFFIN BOOKS

PUFFIN BOOKS

Published by the Penguin Group
Penguin Books Ltd, 80 Strand, London WC2R 0RL, England
Penguin Group (USA), 375 Hudson Street, New York, New York 10014, USA
Penguin Books Australia Ltd, 707 Collins Street, Melbourne, Victoria 3008, Australia
Penguin Group (Canada), 90 Eglinton Avenue East, Suite 700, Toronto, Ontario, Canada M4P 2Y3
Penguin Books India (P) Ltd, 11 Community Centre, Panchsheel Park, New Delhi – 110 017, India
Penguin Group (NZ), 67 Apollo Drive, Rosedale, Auckland 0632, New Zealand
Penguin Books (South Africa) (Pty) Ltd, Block D, Rosebank Office Park,
181 Jan Smuts Avenue, Parktown North, Gauteng 2193, South Africa

Penguin Books Ltd, Registered Offices: 80 Strand, London WC2R 0RL, England

puffinbooks.com

Hairy Maclary From Donaldson's Dairy
First published in New Zealand by Mallinson Rendel Publishers Ltd 1983
Published in Picture Puffins 1985
Copyright © Lynley Dodd, 1983
Hairy Maclary's Bone
First published in New Zealand by Mallinson Rendel Publishers Ltd 1984
Published in Picture Puffins 1986
Copyright © Lynley Dodd, 1984
Hairy Maclary Scattercat
First published in New Zealand by Mallinson Rendel Publishers Ltd 1985
Published in Picture Puffins 1987
Copyright © Lynley Dodd, 1985
Hairy Maclary's Caterwaul Caper
First published in New Zealand by Mallinson Rendel Publishers Ltd 1987
Published in Picture Puffins 1989
Copyright © Lynley Dodd, 1987
Hairy Maclary's Rumpus at the Vet
First published in New Zealand by Mallinson Rendel Publishers Ltd 1989
Published in Picture Puffins 1991
Copyright © Lynley Dodd, 1989
This edition first published in New Zealand by Mallinson Rendel Publishers Ltd 1996
Published in Puffin Books in hardback 2002
018
Published in Puffin Books in paperback 2002
4

Copyright © Lynley Dodd, 1983, 1984, 1985, 1987, 1989, 1996

Made and Printed in China

British Library Cataloguing in Publication Data
A CIP catalogue record for this book is available from the British Library

ISBN Hardback 978-0-670-91386-2
ISBN Paperback 978-0-141-31594-2

CONTENTS

Hairy Maclary
from Donaldson's Dairy

Out of the gate
and off for a walk
went Hairy Maclary
from Donaldson's Dairy

and Hercules Morse
as big as a horse

with Hairy Maclary
from Donaldson's Dairy.

Bottomley Potts
covered in spots,
Hercules Morse
as big as a horse

and Hairy Maclary
from Donaldson's Dairy.

Muffin McLay
like a bundle of hay,
Bottomley Potts
covered in spots,
Hercules Morse
as big as a horse

and Hairy Maclary
from Donaldson's Dairy.

Bitzer Maloney
all skinny and bony,
Muffin McLay
like a bundle of hay,
Bottomley Potts
covered in spots,
Hercules Morse
as big as a horse

and Hairy Maclary
from Donaldson's Dairy.

Schnitzel von Krumm
with a very low tum,
Bitzer Maloney
all skinny and bony,
Muffin McLay
like a bundle of hay,
Bottomley Potts
covered in spots,
Hercules Morse
as big as a horse

and Hairy Maclary
from Donaldson's Dairy.

With tails in the air
they trotted on down
past the shops and the park
to the far end of town.
They sniffed at the smells
and they snooped at each door,
when suddenly,
out of the shadows
they
saw …

SCARFACE CLAW
the toughest Tom
in
town.

"EEEEEOWWWFFTZ!"
said Scarface Claw.

Off with a yowl
a wail and a howl,
a scatter of paws
and a clatter of claws,
went Schnitzel von Krumm
with a very low tum,
Bitzer Maloney
all skinny and bony,
Muffin McLay
like a bundle of hay,
Bottomley Potts
covered in spots,
Hercules Morse
as big as a horse

and Hairy Maclary
from Donaldson's Dairy,

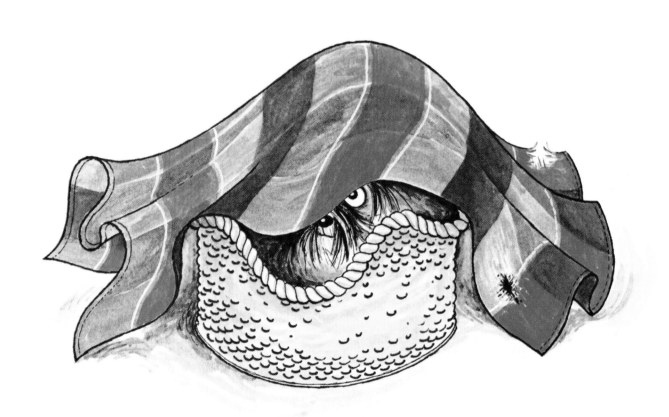

straight back home
to bed.

Hairy Maclary's Bone

Down in the town
by the butcher's shop door,
sat Hairy Maclary
from Donaldson's Dairy.

Out of the door
came Samuel Stone.
He gave Hairy Maclary
his tastiest
bone.

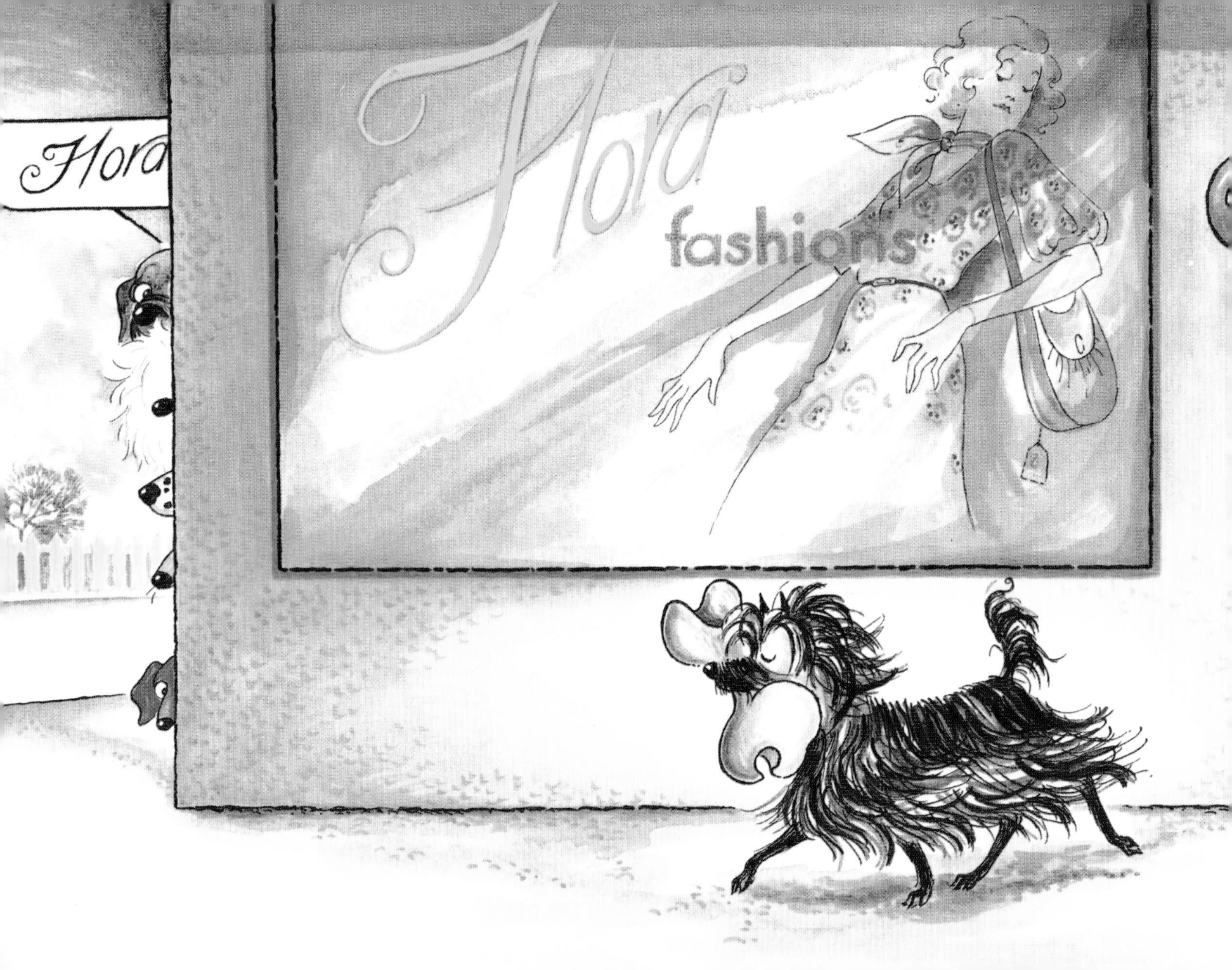
Flora
Flora
fashions

Then off up the street
on scurrying feet,
on his way to the dairy
went Hairy Maclary.

And chasing him home,
with their eyes on the bone,
went Hercules Morse,
Bottomley Potts,
Muffin McLay,
Bitzer Maloney
and Schnitzel von Krumm
with the very low tum.

Hungrily sniffing
and licking their chops,
they followed him up
past the school and the shops.

They came to the sign
selling Sutherland's Sauce.
Through they all went —

except Hercules Morse.

They came to a hedge
along Waterloo Way.
Under they went —

except Muffin McLay.

They came to a yard
full of dinghies and yachts.
Round they all went —

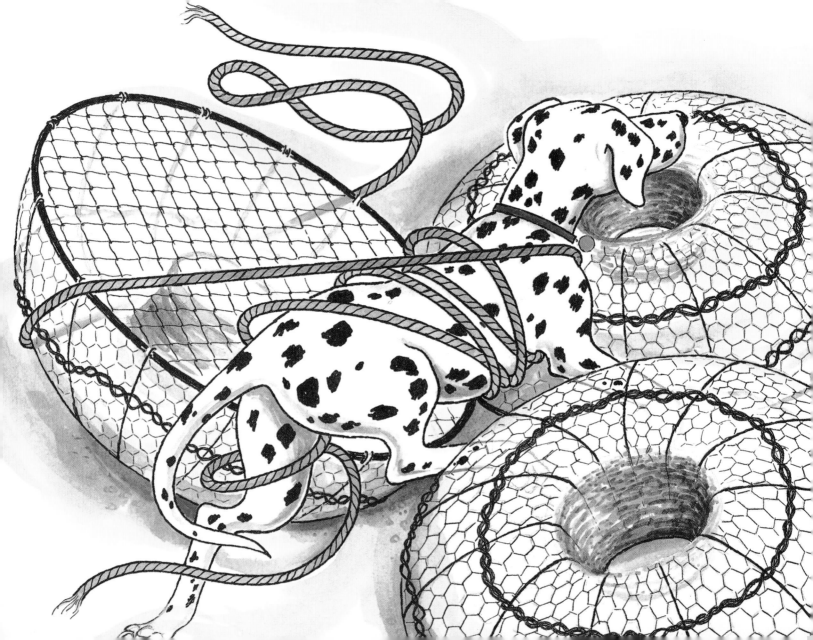

except Bottomley Potts.

They came to a building site,
cluttered and stony.
Over they went —

except Bitzer Maloney.

They came to a wall
by the house of Miss Plum.
One of them jumped —

but not Schnitzel von Krumm.

So at last he was free
to go home on his own,
Hairy Maclary
with ALL of his
bone.

Hairy Maclary Scattercat

Hairy Maclary
felt bumptious and bustly,
bossy and bouncy
and frisky and hustly.
He wanted to run.
He wanted to race.
But the MAIN thing he wanted
was something
to
chase.

Greywacke Jones
was hunting a bee.

BUT ALONG CAME HAIRY MACLARY …

and chased her up high
in the sycamore tree.

Butterball Brown
was washing a paw.

BUT ALONG CAME HAIRY MACLARY …

and bustled him under
a rickety door.

Pimpernel Pugh
was patting a ball.

BUT ALONG CAME HAIRY MACLARY …

and chased her away
over Pemberton's wall.

Slinky Malinki
was down in the reeds.

BUT ALONG CAME HAIRY MACLARY …

and hustled him into
a drum full of weeds.

Mushroom Magee
was asleep on a ledge.

BUT ALONG CAME HAIRY MACLARY …

and chased her away
through a hole in the hedge.

Down on the path
by an old wooden rail,
twitching a bit,
was the tip of a tail.
With a bellicose bark
and a boisterous bounce,
Hairy Maclary
was ready
to
POUNCE

BUT AROUND CAME SCARFACE CLAW …

who bothered
and bustled him,
rustled and hustled him,
raced him
and chased him

ALL the way
home.

Hairy Maclary's caterwaul caper

With a twitch of his tail
and a purposeful paw,
down by the river
crept Scarface Claw.

He woke up a lizard,
he startled a bee,
and he bothered a blackbird
high in a tree.

Higher and higher
he sneakily snuck,
but up in the branches
he suddenly
STUCK.
'WROWWW-W-W-W-W-W-W,'
he yowled.

Hairy Maclary
was eating his meal;
jellymeat,
biscuits,
a snippet of veal.
All of a sudden
he heard a STRANGE sound;
a yowling,
a wailing
that echoed around,
'*WROWWW-W-W-W-W-W-W.*'
'*YAP-YAP-YAP,*'
said Hairy Maclary,
and off he went.

Hercules Morse
was asleep in a glade,
with his tail in the sun
and his head in the shade.
THEN came the sound
that echoed around,
'*WROWWW-W-W-W-W-W-W.*'
'*WOOF,*'
said Hercules Morse,
and off he went.

Bottomley Potts
was rolling about,
with his feet in the air
and his tongue hanging out.
THEN came the sound
that echoed around,
'*WROWWW-W-W-W-W-W-W.*'
'*RO-RO-RO-RO-RO,*'
said Bottomley Potts,
and off he went.

Muffin McLay
was having a bath,
in the old wooden tub
at the side of the path.
THEN came the sound
that echoed around,
'*WROWWW-W-W-W-W-W-W.*'
'*RUFF-RUFF,*'
said Muffin McLay,
and off he went.

Bitzer Maloney
was having a scratch,
as he lay in the sun
in the strawberry patch.
THEN came the sound
that echoed around,
'*WROWWW-W-W-W-W-W-W.*'
'*BOW-WOW-WOW-WOW,*'
said Bitzer Maloney,
and off he went.

Schnitzel von Krumm
was digging a hole,
in his favourite spot
by the passionfruit pole.
THEN came the sound
that echoed around,
'WROWWW-W-W-W-W-W-W.'
'YIP-YIP,'
said Schnitzel von Krumm,
and off he went.

Puffing and panting
impatient to see,
together they came
to the foot of the tree.
They sniffed and they snuffled,
they bustled around,
and they saw WHAT was making
the terrible sound.

'*YIP-YIP,*'
said Schnitzel von Krumm.
'*BOW-WOW-WOW-WOW,*'
said Bitzer Maloney.
'*RUFF-RUFF,*'
said Muffin McLay.
'*RO-RO-RO-RO-RO,*'
said Bottomley Potts.
'*WOOF,*'
said Hercules Morse.
'*YAP-YAP-YAP,*'
said Hairy Maclary
and …

'WROWWW-W-W-W-W-W-W,'
said Scarface Claw.
The din was so awful
that up hill and down,
you could hear the CACOPHONY
all over town.

Miss Plum brought a ladder
and climbed up the tree.
She rescued old Scarface;
at last he was free.

With a flick of his tail
and a shake of each paw,
off at a gallop
went Scarface Claw.

And back to their business
and Donaldson's Dairy,
went all of the others
with Hairy Maclary.

Hairy Maclary's Rumpus at the Vet

Down at the Vet's
there were all kinds of pets,
with troubles and woes
from their ears to their toes.
Sniffles and snuffles
and doses of flu,
itches and stitches
and tummy ache too.
So many animals,
watchful and wary,
and Hairy Maclary
from Donaldson's Dairy.

There were miserable dogs,
cantankerous cats,
a rabbit with pimples
and rickety rats.
Mice with the sneezes,
a goat in a rage,
and Cassie the cockatoo
locked in her cage.

Cassie had claws
and a troublesome beak.
She saw something twitch
so she gave it a
TWEAK.

She pulled it so hard
that she plucked out a hair
and Hairy Maclary
jumped high in the air.

A bowl full of mice
was bundled about.
Over it went
and the mice tumbled out.

Four fussy budgies
with Grandmother Goff
flew out of their cage
when the bottom dropped off.

Grizzly MacDuff
with a bottlebrush tail
leaped out of his basket
and over the rail.

The Poppadum kittens
from Parkinson Place
squeezed through an opening
and joined in the chase.

Barnacle Beasley
forgot he was sore.
He bumbled and clattered
all over the floor.

Then Custard the labrador,
Muffin McLay
and Noodle the poodle
decided to play.
They skidded and scampered,
they slid all around
and bottles and boxes
came tumbling down.

What a kerfuffle,
a scramble of paws,
a tangle of bodies,
a jumble of jaws.
With squawking and yowling
and mournful miaow,
they really were making
a TERRIBLE row.

Out came the Vet.
'I'll fix them,' she said.
But she tripped on a lead
and fell over instead.

Geezer the goat
crashed into a cage.
He butted the bars
in a thundering rage.

Cassie got mad.
She rattled her beak.
She saw something twitch
so she
gave
it
a ...